MW01148729

This book ~~belongs to:~~
is shared with

_____

_____

_____

we are circle people

to all who connect

© 2018 Conscious Stories LLC

Illustrations by Alexis Aronson

Published by
Conscious Stories LLC
1831 12th Avenue South, Ste 118
Nashville, TN, 37203

Legally speaking all rights are
reserved, so this book may not be
reproduced without the express
written consent of the publisher.
On a relational level, this book can
be read to inspire, engage and
connect parents and children. That is
what it was made for, so please read
the story and be kind enough to give
a mention to Andrew Newman and
The Conscious Bedtime Story Club™

www.consciousstories.com

First Edition
Library of Congress
Control Number: 2017901959
ISBN 978-1-943750-13-9

The last 20 minutes of every day are precious.

Dear parents, teachers, and readers,

Did you know that paired breathing is the fastest way to create a connection with someone? That is why this bedtime story starts with an easy breathing meditation. It is specially designed to help you settle and connect with yourself and your children.

● Please set your intention for calm, open connection. Then start your story time with the **Snuggle Breathing Meditation**. Read each line aloud while taking slow deep breaths together.

● At the end of the story you will find **The Circle Feeling**. The discussion points on this reflection page are crafted to create feelings of belonging. By talking through the day in this way you give your children the opportunity to share moments of loneliness they may have felt. This provides you the opportunity to balance those painful moments with your nourishing connection before they go to sleep.

Enjoy snuggling into togetherness!

Snuggle Breathing

Let's begin our story by breathing together.
Say each line aloud and then
take a slow, deep breath in and out.

I breathe for me.

I breathe for you.

I breathe for us.

I breathe for all that surrounds us.

There was once a Square Village where the Square People lived.

On market day the farmers came from square farms to set up square tables in the market square.

Everything fit neatly side-by-side, and all seemed well.

Then one day a Visitor arrived.

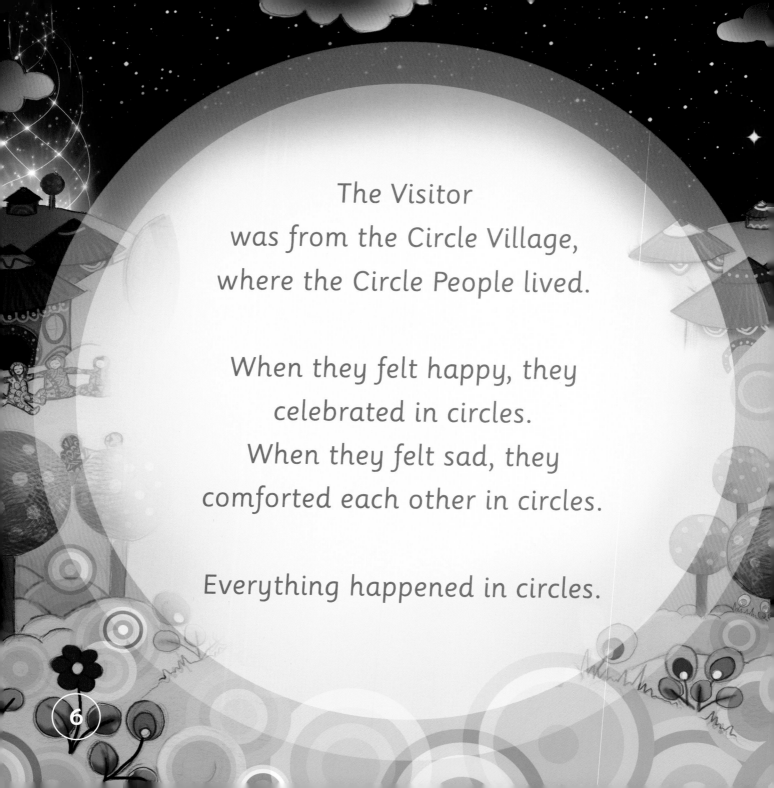

The Visitor
was from the Circle Village,
where the Circle People lived.

When they felt happy, they
celebrated in circles.
When they felt sad, they
comforted each other in circles.

Everything happened in circles.

The Visitor liked the Square Village.
It was neater than the Circle Village.

Everything had its place,
but the Square People
didn't seem happy.

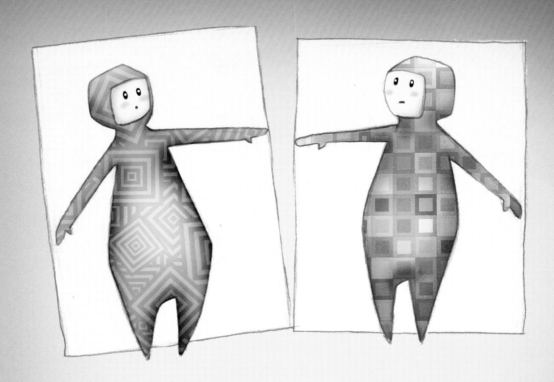

Their hands didn't quite touch.
Their hearts didn't quite connect
and they all seemed very lonely.

The Visitor felt sad.

That night the Visitor dreamed
of home.

He missed sitting close together
with his family and friends.

Close enough to hold hands
and bump knees.

10

Close enough to rest heads on shoulders.

Close enough to feel each other's heartbeat.

In the Circle Village no one ever felt lonely.

As evening fell on the next day an unfamiliar song echoed across the Square Village.

The villagers paused and turned to see the Visitor standing in the center of the market square.

He was singing, with his staff lifted high into the sky.

Music seemed to fall
like beautiful raindrops,
filling the Square People
with curiosity as they
gazed up to the heavens.

14

As the Visitor finished singing,
he struck the ground three times.

Seconds later the earth rumbled
and a large hole appeared.

Inside was a long-forgotten fire circle,
filled with dry wood
just waiting to be set on fire.

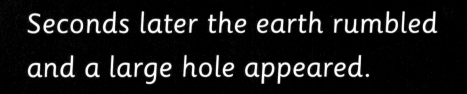

With one prayer of hope
and one strike of a match,
the fire roared to life.

As the fire's warmth radiated
through the village,
the pointed corners of the Square People
began to round and soften.

20

One by one, their
hands reached out,

first touching,
then holding...

23

Smiles appeared,
followed by giggles and laughter,
until soon the whole Square
Village was singing, dancing,
and sharing...

hand-in-hand in a circle
around the fire.

How strong are your circles?

As you look back over your day, sit close enough to hold hands and bump knees, close enough to rest heads on shoulders, and close enough to feel each other's heartbeat.

It is time to create that circle feeling.

Reflect on your day

The Circle Feeling

2

What does a circle moment feel like to you?

1

What does a square moment feel like to you?

3

Tell me about a square moment when your hearts didn't quite connect. What did you do to grow connection?

4

Tell me about a circle moment when you felt very connected. Who was in your circle?

5

Before we go to sleep, let's send love to everyone we shared our day with.

the laughing witch

how diablo became Spirit

Anna Breytenbach & Andrew Newman

the tree of goodness

Andrew Newman

Rolling Thunder finds his herd

Andrew Newman

the elephant who tried to tiptoe

the boy who searched for silence

Andrew

the dad who didn't know

Andrew Newman

we are circle people

Andrew Newman

the hug who got stuck

And

the sunburnt polar bear

the fish who searched for water

Andrew Newman

a little light

the bee who could not choose her flower

Andrew Newman

the prayer who searched for God

Andrew Newman

the girl with waterfall eyes

Andrew N

the forgetful elephant

Andrew Newman

the collection

The Conscious Bedtime Story Club

snuggling into togetherness

Conscious Bedtime Stories

A collection of stories with wise and lovable characters who teach spiritual values to your children

Helping you connect more deeply in the last 20 minutes of the day

Stories with purpose

Lovable characters who overcome life's challenges to find peace, love and connection.

Reflective activity pages

Cherish open sharing time with your children at the end of each day.

Simple mindfulness practices

Enjoy easy breathing practices that soften the atmosphere and create deep connection when reading together.

Supportive parenting community

Join a community of conscious parents who seek connection with their children.

Free downloadable coloring pages
Visit www.consciousstories.com

 #consciousbedtimestories   @Conscious Bedtime Story Club

29

Andrew Newman - author

Andrew Newman is the award-winning author and founder of www.ConsciousStories.com, a growing series of bedtime stories purpose-built to support parent-child connection in the last 20 minutes of the day. His professional background includes deep training in therapeutic healing work and mindfulness. He brings a calm yet playful energy to speaking events and workshops, inviting and encouraging the creativity of his audiences, children K-5, parents, and teachers alike.

Andrew has been an opening speaker for Deepak Chopra, a TEDx presenter in Findhorn, Scotland and author-in-residence at the Bixby School in Boulder, Colorado. He is a graduate of The Barbara Brennan School of Healing, a Non-Dual Kabbalistic healer and has been actively involved in men's work through the Mankind Project since 2006. He counsels parents, helping them to return to their center, so they can be more deeply present with their kids.

TEDˣ **"Why the last 20 minutes of the day matter"**

Alexis Aronson — illustrator

Alexis is a self-taught illustrator, designer and artist from Cape Town, South Africa. She has a passion for serving projects with a visionary twist that incorporate image making with the growth of human consciousness for broader impact. Her media range from digital illustration and design to fine art techniques, such as intaglio printmaking, ceramic sculpture, and painting. In between working for clients and creating her own art for exhibition, Alexis is an avid nature lover, swimmer, yogi, hiker, and gardener.

www.alexisaronson.com

Star Counter

Every time you breathe together and read aloud, you make a star shine in the night sky.

Color in a star to count how many times you have read this book.